Springhorn
Fairy Tales
& Verse

By
David Springhorn

Library of Congress
ISBN 978-0-9817143-6-6

Copyright © David A. Springhorn, 2009

First Edition; December, 2009

Ion Drive Publishing
IonDrivePublishing.com

Dedicated to
My Family...

Ye Contents

The Lady of the Lake

The dawn gave birth to two waiting shapes in the mist, beside a lake so still, the vain night could have used it for a mirror. One of them was an old man, his face haggard, his eyes deep and full of history. The other was a boy, nearly a man, wearing the uncomfortable shell of a king: armor with high-polished devices of ancient family power. He wore a crown so new, it dripped polish upon the rich velvet of his tunic.

"Merlin," he whined, "I've prayed till my mail cut my knees up. Why won't you tell me why we're here?"

The old man smiled fondly, "Come now, Arthur. This is the moment I've waited for since I first saw it in the stars. Let me savor it before you take it for your own." Even on this cold morning, Merlin felt the warmth of expectation. He waited for a miracle.

That miracle lived beneath the lake, in a blue green chamber carved from a wave, made into a hall decorated with jade-like bas-reliefs of a thousand magical beasts, gods, and sprites, all of her acquaintance, All were frozen betwixt one moment and the next, for she was a mistress of time itself. The pure moment was her realm. She sat on a throne of freshwater pearls set in rosy coral. In her lap lay a long sword. She sharpened it with an ancient dragon's tooth. The blade had been deadly sharp a moment before, but now was a key to open the doors of hell for anyone who stood before it.

The hilt was made to look like a soaring griffin ready to strike. Down the blade, ancient runes proclaimed that he who wielded it was Britain's true king. A fair countenance was reflected in the bright steel. Her hair rippled as a waterfall over golden stones and parted to reveal a face so young, it seemed unfit to be set in such an earnest frown. Her eyes were large and serene.

Sparks flew from her last ringing stroke. Then her face became springtime. "Here is a sword worthy of a new king," she purred. "It will sever the last embrace of chaos, and the land, for a time, will gush peace." She swung it wide and split the throne like a flock of soap bubbles. She laughed a lady's laugh of triumph. How long had she sharpened it? A day, a year, a hundred thousand?

It was given into her hands by the Green Man, the guardian spirit of the island. At the first glance, he was a man, but at the second one saw him as a wild concoction of vines, flowers, and moss, wound over a skeleton of young branches and reeds. His leafy face bore eyes like the pools one finds in the deepest part of the woods. He was the herald of the earth, made to plead for her to the race of men. He came to her lake and called to her with his great oaken hunting horn, born alive, as was he, from the gigantic soul-tree at England's heart.

"Take this," he said with a voice as sweet as forest wind. "It is a shard of the great war hammer of terrible, thundering Thor, once our Patron God. The splinter fell when He smote the ground to sever our island from the mainland to make Him a private garden to stroll and be gentle in. He is gone now to the pits of nothing, with all his godish clan. He left us this enchanted iron to forge a weapon of defense against those that worship death and greed. It was born of fire and of the earth; I have cooled it with the wind. Now, you must shape it with water, a single drop at a time. Then shall you give this to the boy king, and he shall imbue it with his soul and spirit and so bring it to life."

The Green Man bowed and bestowed the sword, then making a deeper bow, took three steps back into the trees and was made one with them. When first it came to her, it had been rough as stone. She'd shaped it with her mind and the patient water of her lake until, moment after

3

moment, drop by drop, it turned it into a work of shining wonder.

She marveled as it shone in her hand, saying, "Here is a scythe to mow down ignorance and reap the harvest of pure true chivalry." Her voice rose. "We shall have a king pure of heart, honest and true. Though I can see how he will die for his dreams, he will inspire all men, giving them the gift of real peace." She sighed. "Now, it's off to the world of moving time, where the humans slog against the drowning current of eternity."

With one swift pass of her hand, the palace was liquid. Suspended in the emerald depths, the weapon glowed deep green and deadly. She sang one high note that churned the water all about her like unto a glittering galaxy. Then, thrusting the blade before her, she shot off faster than thought, almost vanishing, breaking the surface into a crown of flashing foam. Her arm appeared, a pedestal of ivory. Her hand gripped the hilt with the very strength of time itself. The upheld blade caught the dawn like fire. The miracle had arrived.

The old man cried, "Behold, Arthur! This is your sword, Excalibur."

The Court of Fire

Perith was the wizard Loth's apprentice.

"When will it end?" he whined, approaching the pig sty. "When I was a squire, I never knew how foul a hog wallow could be." He lifted a giant bucket of slop, so putrid his eyes smarted. He was a sturdy boy of fifteen, but still had to grunt and struggle with the great half-barrel. "If I'd known what they rolled in, I'd a never eaten pork. Magic is so glamorous."

The giant hog charged the fence and snarled in a bloodthirsty, hoggish fashion. Perith jumped back, saying, "Oh, I shall feast upon your haunch, you Demon swine." The pig, enraged, shook his head from side to side, covering the boy with slop-infested slobber.

Perith raised the empty barrel above his head to bash the hog's skull in. "Ham for dinner!" he shouted. The barrel stopped, wrenched itself from his hands, and after completing a beautiful arc, settled itself on his head. In vain, Perith struggled to pull it off, until ever so slowly, the bucket raised itself. Revealing nothing.

He looked about him. No one, just the

wizard's tower, a bunch of half-timbered sheds, the pen, strutting fowl and… a floating staff? Which proceeded to beat him about the head and shoulders, then pushed him through the tower door. The staff hopped to the hand of a round, middle-aged man, Loth the Mighty (though he didn't look it). He wore a green velvet wizard's robe, festooned with a dirty apron. He watched a cauldron closely.

"Casting our future?" said Perith, at a loss.

"Cooking our dinner." The man gestured, and an onion rose, quartered itself, and plunged into the soup. "Been worrying the hog again," Loth smirked. A small vegetable, with little root arms and legs, dived into the pot.

Perith winced. "Mandrake root, ugh!"

"It will help your second sight. You need it." The wizard continued, "It'll be awhile 'till food is ready. Go to the trance hut, and build a fire." A leg of something spun itself apart and fell into the pot. "Light a candle and go under. Gaze at the flame. It will keep you busy 'till we eat, and wash up. You smell like hog's vomit."

Perith did as he was told. The water was cold. Then, on to the shack. Perith was about to go in, when he heard his master yell: "Don't forget to close the door!"

6

The boy muttered, "On a day like this, who wouldn't?" He went to a plank table, got out a wax candle, then whipped his hand over a pile of logs in the fire pit. With a word of power, the logs started to smoke. Perith gagged, then shouted at the top of his lungs. The wood exploded, and he had to run about, putting out sparks.

He sat on an old chair, lit the candle, and peered into the little flame. The room went all wavy (he was good at trances), and soon the room was nothing but candle flame. All of a sudden, he noticed that there was a door shape in the flame. The more he concentrated, the clearer it became: A golden pulsing door, with a lock and key. He turned the key. The door swung open into a stone courtyard. There was a hall, with a great black door that smelled of charcoal. He opened it and looked into a dazzling light. As it calmed down, he beheld a long hall of scorched rock, lit with what seemed to be candle-holders glowing red as a forge. Beautiful music filled the humid air. Minstrels played on brass fiddles and lutes. A circle of tall, beautiful folk dressed in satins of red, gold, and silver glided around a giant of a man who was calling the steps. He wore what seemed to be a crystal crown, set with raw amber and rubies. They danced as if upon the stifling air.

7

A beautiful maiden noticed him. Her hair was sunshine, and if the sea could burn, that was the color of her eyes. She held out her hand. Perith gulped and took it. She began to spin him around. Faster and faster, he lost himself in her gaze, so much so, he didn't notice the musicians inching toward the door and out into the courtyard. The dancers followed, leaping and capering through the golden door.

They danced all about the hut till the place glowed. The woman grabbed Perith and kissed him. He couldn't breathe, and then...

A great wind swept the dancers away. As the maiden sailed back through the golden door, she blew him a kiss that trailed off into curling smoke. Then it slammed shut. Something hit him across the face. The next thing he knew, he was standing in a ring of glowing coals. The shed was gone, the candle snuffed, and his clothes were smoking.

His master stood before him, smiling, his smoldering staff in his hand. "You've met the fairy court of fire. I told you to close the door. They came into our world and nearly burned you alive." He pointed. "Look at that log! You can still see them dancing in the embers." The wizard patted his shoulder. "They like you," the wizard said, pushing him toward the tower. "You'll be able to gain wisdom from their king and a lot more from their queen, if you take my meaning." He dug an elbow into his ribs. "By the way, don't kiss her outside of the door. She'll smother you." He smacked him hard on the back and said, "Tonight, we celebrate with wine! Tomorrow, you can start building another hut, after you tend the pig."

Perith stumbled down the path. "She likes me," he grinned.

The Ride of the Midnight Pooka

*The Pooka is an Irish spirit that causes havoc among mortals
and is beloved of the fairies...*

Shall ever the mind serve itself & be happy
    on a diet of reality?

I know it craves the deep and purple spice
    of madness,

For how else shall it have the strength to see
    the true Pooka?

As she merrily sings the sunlight into golden ribbons

    to bridle the sweet pink piglets,

All for a starlite ride, along the pixie paths
    of glowing silver black.

Who would not trade a tawdry soul
    for secret peeks into the dewy dell,

Where she & elvin minstrels play on instruments
    forged & carved of dreams, of pure delight!

With bass tones given by that self same piglet
    that she loves so well.

For all this mystic haunting music,
    intangible as fairy laughter on the wind,

Is orchestra, to herald in its mighty tinyness,
    the silent coming of the fairy king & queen.

And so they come, astride their steeds, grey mouses,
    dappled brown & perfect proud within their
        pattering steps,

Their bits of purest moonstone shine,
    but not so pulsing vivid as the king & queen,

Who's song is light that mixes with the night
    & so they swoop away,

As if a flock of damsel flies had burst
    out of the new made moon!

'Till all is dark green silent dripping leaves,
    & shining eyes! for last to go is Pooka,

Who, with perfect curtsey makes obeisance
    to the little pig,

And with a silly giggle, she disappears into a puff
    of violet fairystars, to ride the silken evening
        into dreams.

For such a sight a human certainly would sacrifice
    his soul, but all the Pooka asks is true belief..

The Old Troll

there was a troll so bad and bold,
when he was younger, so I'm told.
an evil brute with thundering roar
devouring billy-goats & gore.

now, it's mushroom, root, and nut;
his great paw gathers nothing but.
cooked or fried, jellied, raw
all tumble down his gaping maw.

the finest fruit, the truffle dark
are his dessert, but look! oh hark!

a fairy maid comes fluttering by
like dew and starlight in the sky
her Opel wings all streaked with gold
pulse quick as winks, joy to behold.

her silver tresses flying free,
her Ivory skin glows saucily

a little spark pops in troll's soul
as dark as any rabbit's hole.
tho he eats fodder, sure he'd trade
all vegetables for fairy maid

for in his evil days he'd feast
on unicorn & questing beast,
elves and pixies, goblin foul
the thought made his great stomach growl.

but fairy maid! the best of all
a tasty little fem fatale!

ah,

to nibble on her tiny feet,
to munch her legs so rich and sweet;
make sandwiches out of her wings
with fillings made of other things.

he starts to slather, belch and drool
he chases her; oh, what a fool,
for she's as swift as rays of dawn
she sparkles off, he stumbles on

but always just beyond his reach
she leads him to a river's beach
where forest thins to river bank
there fairies cluster rank on rank

singing laughing see him stare
at clouds of sparkles in the air;

he lunges in, they squeak and fly,
"come here my meal, prepare to die!"
the old troll bellows to this throng
he twists and hops; they lead him on

into the flow, till all at once
they trip him up to fall, poor dunce.
a thousand maids, each a jewel
laugh as he wallows in a pool

he starts to float, the fairies land
on knee and leg and chest and hand.

the fairest one, (no doubt the queen)
lands on his nose to view the scene
"old troll, do you feel better now?"
he nods his head (he cannot bow).

she sez, "musicians, fiddles bring,
to serenade this silly thing."
the minstrels perch upon his brow,
"let's start our fairy revels now."

the queen commands, they start to sing,
and play until the rafters ring.
the dancers spin, they leap and charge,
he floats, like Cleopatra's barge.

and as the dusk beholds these sights,
he glows with many thousand lights.
the Old Troll sighs and smiles a smile
that stretches out about a mile,

and sez

"tho it must always end the same,
I must admit I love this game."
as he sails off upon his back
he's quite forgot his fairy snack

The Fairy Moon

The moon was bright and beautiful,
The mists passed over secretly.
The glens were jeweled in midnight dew,
That caught the moonlight dreamily.

The silence was as soft as sighs,
The evening, light and lingering,
And in a thicket green and deep
The wizard sat expectantly.

Each autumn moon would find him there,
Beside a pool of silver blue.
To wait and watch a miracle
That few had sight to gaze upon.

The fireflies danced trippingly,
Each one a tiny lantern made.
And to the sight of mortal men
It was a pond and nothing more.

The sorcerer took up his staff,
And waved it thrice before his eyes,
Then spoke an incantation low.
And in a moment all was changed.

Each light became a courtier,
Whose tiny eyes glowed cheerily.
Some rode upon a dragonfly.
While others floated in the air.

The dew was changed to dancing maids,
Who played upon stalks of grass.
They seemed to all wait patiently
For what the wizard longed to see.

And then the northern star appeared.
The small light shone within the pool
And spun into a blazing fire
That nearly took the wizard's sight.

And from the centre of this blaze
As if out of a dragon's egg.
There stepped a lady glowing bright
As if of moonlight she was made.

The fairy throng cheered joyfully,
And all about her dancing flew,
As if they were the milky way
She, center of the universe.

Her skin was silk and ivory pale.
Her eyes were deep and fairy wise.
Dark golden hair flowed like a brook
That rippled past her shoulders bare.

She spoke no words to all her court,
And yet they seemed to understand.
For some flew off to tasks unknown,
While others sat there listening.

And as the fairies held their court,
The wizard rose and with his staff
He traced a mighty pentagram,
That caused a wind to swirl about.

It took the court like autumn leaves,
That scattered them far and away.
He then spoke words of subtle power,
That trembled in the midnight air.

Then filaments like spider silk
Wound round about the fairy queen.
That fed upon her silver light
Till strongly was she bound and caught.

"Release me now, oh mortal fool"
Her rage burned slowly in her eyes,
"You know not who you're dealing with
Or else in terror would you flee."

"I mistress am of light and fire,
And when I burst these paltry bonds
I'll sear the flesh off of your bones.
And feed it to the ogres fell."

"My band shall raise you off the ground,
And carry you far from the shore
And there beneath the roaring waves
 Shall always dwell forever more."

The wizard listened to her speech,
But both did know it was in vain.
His wards were made of all his power
His magic kept her in his thrall

Her face grew sad till tear drops fell
And where they landed flowers grew
"Oh mortal man, what would you have?
My powers are at your command."

"Will you have silver gold or gems
Or secrets of my fairy realm.
I'll make you lord of dreamer's land,
And you shall know mans' every thought"

"The unicorn I'll catch for you
And touch his horn upon your breast,
So shall you live eternally,
All will I do for my release."

The wizard stood and cleared his throat
And slightly trembling spoke these words;
"I do not wish to take with force
These gifts you offer up to me."

"I've studied you for all my life
Since I a young apprentice was,
Magic bent entirely
To bind you into slavery"

"I watched you, though you never knew,
Awake the flowers in the spring.
In lovers dreams in summertime
I saw you deepen all their joy"

In winter you would use your light
To guide the frightened traveler.
And lead them safely to their homes,
All have I seen and marveled at."

"But best it is in autumn time
I've sat and wondered at your skill.
You put the forest all to rest
And guard it all the winter long."

"So long I've labored for this chance
To bind you with my magic spell
I have one boon to ask of you
Which now I fear you cannot do."

The fairy stood and braced herself
To feel the blow she knew would come
The wizard kneeled upon the ground
And shyly said these very words.

"Love me lady, love me please,"
He stammered in embarrassment.
"As time has passed my heart is yours
My every thought belongs to you."

"I know I cannot force your love
No vow or magic does exist.
To force you to that tender place
Where I would have you join with me"

"Look in my heart, behold my soul,
For both are true oh this I swear
My powers, magic, I'll renounce
If you would simply smile at me."

"I saw you love a mortal man
My heart was filled with jealousy
It ended and I was reborn
And empty hope again was mine."

"I cannot fly upon the breeze
Or follow you to fairy halls.
I cannot be a fairy king
And be eternal lord to you.

"But I can pledge my staff and books
My life to you, and fealty
I would serve in slavery
If pity you would take on me."

The wizard then took up his staff,
It slashed the air with magic fire,
He said one word the webs were gone
And so the fairy queen was free.

The sorcerer bent down his head
Awaiting doom to fall on him
He had sincerely spoke his piece
And he was now prepared to die.

There was no sound but cricket call
And peals of laughter like to bells
And light like daylight and a voice
Said, "Raise yourself, beloved fool."

He saw her in her majesty
The grove with fairy glamour shone
Her troupe of fairies fluttering
About the pool and rocks and trees.

The fairy queen did softly smile
The wizard nearly lost his breath
She quieted the fairy host
And in a voice of velvet said.

"I've gazed into your mage's soul
And found it true as tempered steel
Such love is not a trifling gift
So I accept it as it is."

"I'll come to you in winter snows,
In golden days of summer time.
In greenest spring we'll walk and speak
In autumn by this very pool."

"For these four days you'll know my love
And I will call you when 'tis time
I will belong to only you
Until the second midnight chime."

"Farewell my love till winter comes"
She kissed her hand in fond adieu
Then all the lights revolved and flashed
And all was silent in the glade.

The wizard stood in mute delight
A knowing smile upon his face
Content with all that had transpired
And yearning for the winter snow.

The Hook & Peter Song

*This song was composed
by the lost boys of Neverland
to the tune of Dickey Duncan...*

Joss Hook he was a buccaneer
Or so the stories tell
The butcher of the Spanish main
Supplying meat to hell
Ol' Peter Pan sez here's a game
For me an' all my band
He stole those pirates & their ship
To play in Neverland

Chorus:
When the moon is like a skull
Be sure your cutlass isn't dull
Call to quarters pirates drumming
Run & hide 'cause Hook is coming

Ol' Capitan Hook he cursed & swore
When he saw what was on
You blasted boy, let go a'me,
I'll never be your pawn
The bloody pirate swung his blade
Pan shot into the sky
Then grimly swept his dagger out
& crowed his battle cry

Chorus

The duel was on, the battle hot
The blades flashed in the air
Though each was dealt a bloody wound
They battled unaware
Then Hook he struck a killing blow
Bold Pan turned it away
Then like a falcon fell his sword
& hacked Hook's hand away

Chorus

When Hook beheld the bloody stump
He screamed to wake the dead
I'll split yer gutz, accursed boy,
I'll part ya from yer head
Up in the blue our Peter Pan
Said catch me if you can
Then like a thunderbolt he fell
Upon that evil man

Chorus

Avast! sez Hook, here's my revenge
I'll gut him like a sow
But at the final minute
Peter halted with a bow
He spied a giant crocodile
Its jaws were open wide
You wouldn't dare, said Captain Hook
Oh yes I would, Pan cried

Chorus

The crocodile sat up & begged
& waged his spiky tail
Pan tossed the hand into its mouth
Ol' Hook began to wail
The croc sat back & licked his chops
As if he liked the treat
Then lovingly he looked at Hook
Like he was sausage meat

Chorus

The crocodile he lunged & snapped
Hook bravely ran away
Through swamp & bog & quicksand
The devil sought his prey
The mighty Capitan swore an oath
Upon his severed hand
He'd kill us all & spill our blood
All over Neverland

Chorus

The Miller's Son

Young Rupert was a millers son,
    and spent his days in clouds of flour;
And he did love the millers trade
    and spent with joy his every hour.
He had a trumpet of a laugh
    that filled the air with mirth and joy,
And everyone from all about
    did dearly love the miller's boy...

One evening when the work was done
    and supper set before the fire,
A Storyman did ply his art
    and he was worthy of his hire.
Such tales of wizards far away
    and fairy kings and dragons flame,
'Till Rupert's mouth was all agape,
    his eyes like barrel-hoops became;
"Beware the little brownie men
    that live beneath this hearth," he said,
"For if you mock their tinyness
    some moonlit night you'll wake up dead!
But worst of all is Oberon
    the fairy king, you'd best beware;

He has a howling goblin court
    that preys on travelers unaware;
His sprites and elves. on crossroads swoop
    to carry off all mortal men,
To ride the wind eternally
    and never more be seen again...

The family shivered in their shoes
    then went to bed to dream and snore,
But Rupert slyly stayed behind
    and quick as winks slipped out the door;
He silently ran through the town
    until upon the crossroads stood;
He tensed in expectation great
    as still as any block of wood,
And just as he had had enough
    and made to go back home to bed,
He heard a noise that pricked his ear
    and filled his heart with frozen dread;
A yowling barking mewling sound
    fell down upon him from the sky,
And then a rush of hellish wind
    came rolling tumbling roaring by;
And all at once that dismal road
    was filled with light from torches bright;

The goblin court had now arrived,
 the haunted travelers of the night.
No two were anyway the same
 some green, some brown, some darkest blue;
Their talons clawed the soggy ground
 most had sharp teeth to slobber through.
Then two foul goblins clamped him tight
 and each of them did drool and moan,
And in a state of rare delight
 did drag him to a carvéd throne...

And there in state sat Oberon,
 bedecked in jewels and velvet rags,
His narrow eyes were golden hued,
 his forehead sported horns of stags;
His fingernails were sharp as fangs,
 his flesh, green as a laurel wreath.
The fairy king then grinned a grin
 that showed a row of pointed teeth;
"Well, by my troth," the monarch said,
 "I see we've caught the chosen one
Unless I much mistaken am
 you are young Rupe the millers son;
You've come to ride the riot wind
 and there become my good right hand,

If not, your future will be bleak;
    I'll feed you to my goblin band."

So Rupert bowed, the monsters cheered,
    and all about him danced and sang;
They offered him a loving cup
    that had a nasty earthy tang;
The liquor went right to his head
    and Rupe began to dance about,
And high above the revelry
    great Oberon began to shout,
"I tire of our revels here;
    we must be off ere break of day
The sun shall never catch us here
    come all my henchmen, Off! Away!
Now Rupert, lad, attend me now,
    for we must fly to foreign shore;
Here is a spell I'll teach you now
    and up into the clouds you'll soar..."

The fairy rose to his full height
    and in a voice of iron, did call,
"IT'S HO! OFF TO THE SCOTTISH MOORS!"
    and they repeated one and all.
The words had hardly left his lips
    when Rupe was lifted off the ground,

32

And cork-screwed madly through the air
    at speeds that set his heart to pound;

For hours on end they chased the moon
    and all the throng was filled with mirth,
'Till all at once they slowed and dropped
    and lightly touched upon the earth...

"My friends, behold the Scottish moor!"
    great Oberon proclaimed with pride,
"We shall take time to feast and drink
    for here the Mountain Kings reside;
Then all at once as if on cue
    the bogs and stones began to rise,
And formed into a crowd of men
    with arms of rock and laughing eyes;
"We welcome you, oh Oberon,"
    a voice like cavern-echoes bawled
"Come drink our brew of liquid stone
    although it might your gullets scald!"

Poor Rupert took his tankard up
    and sadly eyed the steaming cup;
Then tasted it and licked his lips
    and greedily did drink it up.

"We'll dance a fling and jig about,"
    the mountain men began to roar,
"We must be quick for day is nigh
    and dawn is knocking at the door."

They danced a riot, spun and leaped,
    'till daylight peeked into the gloom,
Then Oberon cried, "Forward, men!
    ITS HO! OFF TO THE PHAROAH'S TOMB!"

By now our Rupe was roaring drunk
    and barley now could holler, HO!
He had to catch a goblin's tail
    as he into the air did go.
He fell into the river Nile
    though how he did he didn't know,
And there upon the further bank
    the orange harvest moon did show
A line of giants, copper hued,
    with falcon face and jackal head;
They said, "Foul mortal, you are ours
    for we are keepers of the dead."
"Egyptian gods," said Oberon, "Your ancient
    powers I rebuke!
The lad is mine and so I say,
    IT'S HO! TO THE CELLERS OF THE DUKE!"

They flew like lightning straight to Spain,
    to castles of a great grandee,
And thru a keyhole all were squeezed;
    when Rupe got caught they laughed with glee.

"Behold the Duke of Parma's hoard!
    Wine barrels far as one can see!
We'll drink them dry and he will rage,
    for we will leave no kind of fee!"
They all fell to, each goblin lad,
    until they all were fit to burst;
Whole barrels tipped and guzzled down
    and then again to slake their thirst.
When half the wine was put away,
    bold Oberon was heard too say,
"Once more the sun is chasing us;
    IT'S HO! THE BAY OF MANDELAY!"
The troupe cried "HO!"and off they flew
    to flee the day and chase the night,
But Rupe, too drunk to whisper HO,
    he could not join them in their flight.
Then all at once the great doors burst
    and men at arms came rushing through,
And last the Duke of Parma came,
    his scowling face a purple hue;

"Who are theeez rogues that steals my wine,"
    the Duke in murdered English said,
"Fo when I finds theeez motleyz crew
    I hang them all until they dead!"
They searched the place around about
    and found Rupe snoring in a vat.

The Duke said, "Hope you likes yur drink,
    for now, señor, you swing for that!"
And so it was at crack of dawn,
    poor Rupe in chains was dragged away;
In dungeon deep he sobered up
    and midst his overhang did say,
"IT'S HO TO ENGLAND! SCOTLAND! FRANCE!
    anywhere that isn't jail,
Oh fairy king come save me now,"
    our hero Rupe did sadly wail...

So in the darkest part of dawn
    our lad was thrown into a cart;
The drums did roll, his head did throb,
    the trumpets brayed, his tears did start,
The rope was fitted on his neck,
    the priest came up, last rights to tell,
Rupe said, "I'm church of England, sir,"
    the priest said, smiling, "Go to hell!"

And just as they would spring the trap
    and put an end to this foul show,
He noticed a peculiar man,
    close-hooded in the nearest row;
He wore a mask adorned with horns
    with golden eyeballs painted on;
A grin broke out on Rupert's face;
    that hooded man was OBERON!!!
He cried, "IT'S HO! FOR FAR CATHAY!"
    and in a trice he wasn't there.
Our lad yelled HO! there was a wind;
    the noose swung empty in the air...

And so it was the miller's son
    was by the fairy whisked away,
And traveled all about the world;
    how many places? Who can say...

Magic

The Island of Britain is infested with fairies, but not so much now as in the days of King Arthur Pendragon. Then, magic dripped like honey from every branch, and you couldn't drink from a stream without getting a water sprite up yer nose. The place was thick with boggards, gnomes, and brownies, not to mention the Green Man himself, Lord of All Forests (but that's another story).

The most beautiful (just ask them) wise and powerful of them all is the fairy court of Mathodeia (which in the language of fairy means she who has all the power). They are the glue that holds the whole magic thing together, and they range about like bees all over the island gathering bits of magic. The capital of the fairy world is in the garden of dreams that surrounds the Great Heart Tree, the king of all the oaks of England; there is the most concentrated magic of all, and there Mathodeia keeps her throne. Just like a queen bee, she gathers in all the loose bits of magic the fairies bring to her, and then she shines it all about to all the corners of Britain.

Now one day when she was at the height of

her power, Mathodeia said to herself, "All this is too much work: I need a prime minister." So, Flying up to a walnut tree, she imbued a walnut with a great gob of fairy glamour. As you know, the walnut shell is one of the places where fairy babies grow from little sparks to full blown fairies. Just as Mathodeia had finished bestowing her glamour, she was called away on business and the walnut was left to raise itself.

Now red squirrels don't know magic from a hole in a tree; to them a nut is a nut and the magic radiating from this one made the little fellow's whiskers twitch. He snatched it, and was about to open it, when a hawk, in its' turn, snatched *him* up and flew away. The squirrel struck him on the nose with the nut, and the magic made the hawk sneeze and drop the little fellow and his prize. The squirrel landed (safely) by the side of a stream, knocking the wind out of him, while the walnut bounced into the water and swirled away, buffeted up and down until it was washed up on a sand bank, where it was found by a fluffy brown black cat with green yellow eyes, who began batting it about.

Now fairy magic is allot like catnip, so the kitty got pixilated and rolled the nut all about in a kittenish manner until with one mighty bat the nut flew against a rock and split open, revealing a fully grown blond-headed and quite dizzy fairy girl with light blue eyes and a smile so wide it made the whole world want to smile along with her.

The cat, thinking her a glowing mouse, was about to eat her when it got a good whiff of her magic. Oh, how she rolled and purred and sniffed the fairy, and the fairy returned the favor. When this had gone on a long time, the fairy asked, "Where am I?"

The cat responded, "You are in the realm of me, Mouth Crusher, bane to all mice. But the humans call me Queen Alsatia."

"Then who am I?" the fairy asked.

Now the cat had no intention of telling her she was a fairy and losing such a wonderful toy, so she said, "You are she who is to pretty to eat," (translation from cat, Marrrrgit), "and I am your mother you are my kitten."

"Well then," Margit said, "what is it that kittens do?"

The cat replied, "Obey their mothers and look out for fairies."

"What are they?" Margit puzzled.

The cat thought about it, and said, "Little wingéd things that turn kittens into fairies like themselves and then eat them. I saved you just before they ate you because I am so mighty. That's why you look like one; so we must be careful not to let them find you. Hide whenever you see them. Now come here and have a bath." And with this, the cat licked her clean, getting a lovely dose of magic in the processes, and set out to teach Margit how to be a cat.

Purring and prancing she was good at, but she failed at catching mice. She'd put flower buds in their fur and teach them to dance, much to her mother's embarrassment. She was terrible at lapping milk, and she never seemed to be hungry. But when she was thirsty she drank nectar from the flowers.

Alsatia taught her to stay away from humans, but Margit was curious, and got permission to look at them when they were sleeping.

She didn't think much of the big smelly ones but she loved the kitten humans. She would watch them all night, fly up to their faces, and let them blow her back with their sweet breath. One night she heard one of them crying in their sleep, and so she purred in their ear until they were smiling and happy. Then she found a little pearly thing by the pillow and picked it up. Alsatia said it was a baby fang and touched it with her claw, scratching it.

"This looks a little like a bird's eye" said Margit so she got an old claw from the barn floor and scratched the fang a little more and made a passable sculpture of a bird.

"I'll give it to the kitten," she said, and so she did. The child was amazed and put another one beside his pillow, and when Margit made a portrait of Alsatia's face the child went wild and showed it to his friends, so that they all started to leave their teeth by their pillows.

Margit soon became very busy.

One night, when Margit was fluttering about leaving teeth under pillows (this helped them not to get lost), she fell splat on the ground and ran to her mother, crying. Alsatia knew the jig was up, and had to admit to Margit that she was a fairy and that something was wrong. The cat got very serious: "We must go the Great Heart Oak; that is where all the magic comes from (cats know everything). There must be something wrong." So off they went with Margit perched upon the cat's fluffy head. the fairy girl was amazed by the great wide world and thrilled at every rock stream and tree.

They came to a dark forest so quiet that it raised the fur on Alsatia's head. Moving on, they noticed that the trees seemed to be covered in snow, but when they came closer they saw it was very much like pearly tooth stuff. The trees were filled with hundreds of little fairy sculptures; "Nice work," Margit said.

As they got closer, they saw whole trees turned to stone. Fairies that looked like they had been flying away were stiff upon the ground. But strangest of all was an army of a thousand fairies in silver gold armor, frozen as if in attack.

At the center of the grove under the Heart Tree, which glistened and shone in its pristine whiteness, she saw a beautiful statue of a fairy, in her hand a tiny wand. A winged snake thing was wrapped about her so that it looked like they were locked in mortal combat, and their eyes seemed to be joined together.

Alsatia, spitting and yowling, said, "A BASILISK!!!! Don't look into its' eyes or you will be turned to stone. Mathodeia has been enchanted and all her realm has been bewitched (told you cats know everything). Margit, take that silver shield and put it in front of the snake demon's face: he will see his reflection and be destroyed, but be careful of his eyes."

So, using the coiled snake as a ladder, Margit slowly inched up till she could smell the creature's horrid breath. Then she took the shield and put it up to the deadly eyes. There was a *hissssss*, a scream like every animal in the whole world, and the Basilisk expanded like a balloon. Then, with a great explosion that threw Margit backwards, the nasty thing was no more.

In a trice, all the fairies were released from the spell, and stood about with silly grins upon their faces. Then they all looked at Margit and cheered. She felt two hands lift her up and gently turn her about until she looked into the radiant face of Mathodeia, who said, "You have come to me at last, my counselor, and saved the fairy realm. Will you remain here forever at my side?"

Margit stuttered, "Of course."

The fairy queen smiled. "Any reward you wish, you have but to ask."

Margit thought a bit. "Can my mother stay with me?"

The fairy laughed. "Of course she may. We would be honored to have an all-knowing cat as our counselor as well. If there is anything else you may desire, you have but to ask."

Margit paused. "I must go back to my kittens and say good-bye. I will miss giving them presents and purring them to sleep."

And so Margit returned to the human kittens she loved so well, and kissed each and every one, and sang (that's what purring is) in their ears one last time. As she turned to go, she squeaked, "The teeth! Oh, what will I do about that?"

She was sad, then brightened, and went off to

all the parents' beds and whispered to them "Please leave a token for the kittens under their pillows to remember me." And then she flew away.

As you know, humans haven't the talent to carve a baby tooth, so they took small coins (they have heads on them, you know), and placed them under the pillows of the sleeping children.

And that is how grownups became the tooth fairy, although they are all too modest to admit it

The end

Afterword

We are dancing in the ballroom of the moment,
in the palace of the mind.
When we waltz,
the universe is swirled into a cyclone of energy
as streaming as a dancer's flowing hair.
One more spin,
all is pure light, and yet,
I must stop to kiss your hand...